# Stories
## from
# West Africa

by
## Robert Hull

## Illustrated by
# Tim Clarey

RSVP
RAINTREE
STECK-VAUGHN
P U B L I S H E R S
A Steck-Vaughn Company

Austin, Texas
www.steck-vaughn.com

OTHER MULTICULTURAL STORIES:

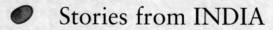

 Stories from THE AMAZON

 Stories from CHINA

Stories from INDIA

 Stories from NATIVE AMERICA

 Stories from THE CARIBBEAN

Published by Raintree Steck-Vaughn Publishers,
an imprint of Steck-Vaughn Company

Library of Congress Cataloging-in-Publication Data
Hull, Robert.
West Africa / Robert Hull.
p.    cm.—(Multicultural stories)
Includes bibliographical references.
ISBN 0-7398-1333-1 (hard)
0-7398-1819-8 (soft)
1. West Africa—Juvenile literature.
[1. West Africa.]
I. Title.  II. Series.

Printed in Italy. Bound in the United States.
1 2 3 4 5 6 7 8 9 0 04 03 02 01 00

# Contents

# Introduction

Africa is huge: a fifth of the land of the Earth is African. The United States would fit into it three times. It has vast areas of desert; thick wet, hot forest; grasslands; and mountains with snow at their tips.

Africa means plains of tall grass, with cattle, elephants, zebras, and buffalo. It means long wide rivers, crocodiles, gorillas, pythons, and tsetse flies. It means oil, cocoa, timber, fine cloths, and—in earlier days—gold, bronze, and silver. It means ancient kingdoms, and fabulous sculptures of wood, bronze, brass, and iron. West Africa means a hundred different peoples, talking many different languages, telling thousands of wonderful stories of flesh-eating ghosts, lying spiders, tricky tortoises, and endless magic.

The stories retold here come from West Africa's English-speaking countries. But the stories existed long before English was spoken there. They were first told in Ashanti or Yoruba or any of the many languages spoken in the region. And they were told long before modern countries like Ghana or Nigeria even existed.

But to make these stories come truly alive, pretend that you're listening to them around an African fire. The night is cool, the stars big and low. The teller leans forward and begins the tale . . .

I hope you enjoy these stories as much as I have.

**Robert Hull**

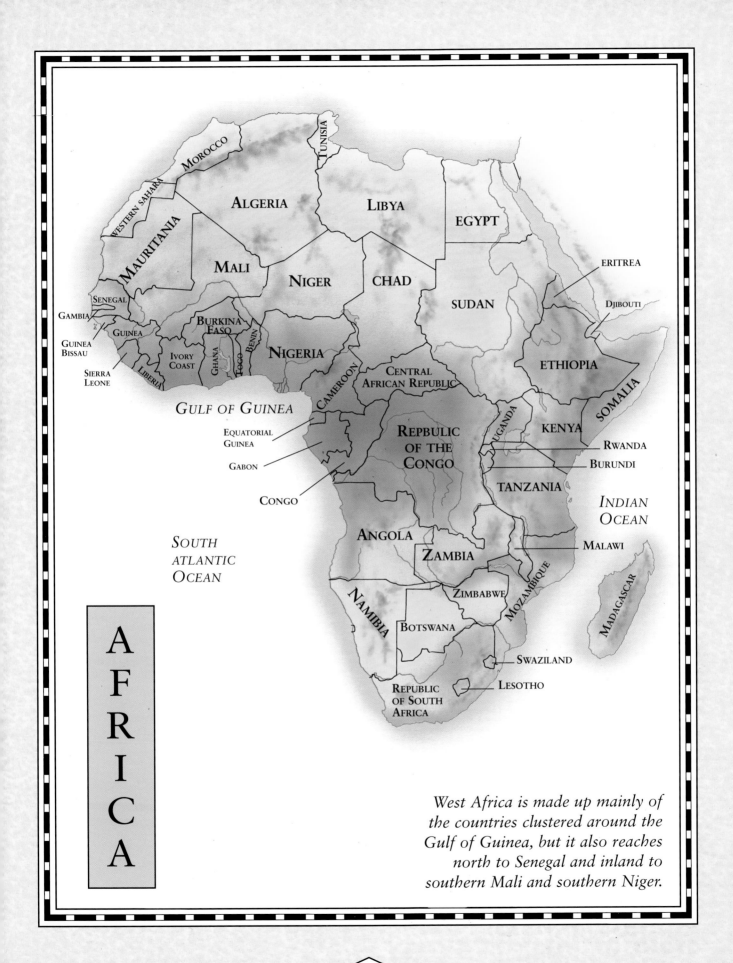

MOROCCO

WESTERN SAHARA

MAURITANIA

ALGERIA

LIBYA

TUNISIA

EGYPT

MALI

NIGER

CHAD

SUDAN

ERITREA

DJIBOUTI

Senegal

GAMBIA

GUINEA

GUINEA BISSAU

SIERRA LEONE

BURKINA FASO

IVORY COAST

GHANA

TOGO

BENIN

LIBERIA

NIGERIA

CAMEROON

CENTRAL AFRICAN REPUBLIC

ETHIOPIA

SOMALIA

GULF OF GUINEA

EQUATORIAL GUINEA

GABON

CONGO

REPBULIC OF THE CONGO

UGANDA

KENYA

RWANDA

BURUNDI

TANZANIA

INDIAN OCEAN

SOUTH ATLANTIC OCEAN

ANGOLA

ZAMBIA

MALAWI

MOZAMBIQUE

MADAGASCAR

ZIMBABWE

NAMIBIA

BOTSWANA

SWAZILAND

LESOTHO

REPUBLIC OF SOUTH AFRICA

# AFRICA

*West Africa is made up mainly of the countries clustered around the Gulf of Guinea, but it also reaches north to Senegal and inland to southern Mali and southern Niger.*

# GHANA

Once, Ghana was a great kingdom. Legend says the king had a hundred horses, and every horse had three servants and a mattress. Ghana's riches came from gold, mined from its forest lands and its rivers. Merchants carried the gold north across the Sahara or took it away by sea. Sculptors made beautiful small boxes for keeping gold in and beautiful tiny gold animals to use as weights—like the gold-finding river crab or the spider.

The spider was a great craftsman too, and a kind of sculptor, and Anansi, a kind of man-spider, became Ghana's favorite story character. He loves gold, power, wisdom, lovely wives, everything—but he's too lazy to work for anything, so he lies and cheats to get what he wants. Sometimes Anansi can actually be helpful, but you rarely know whether he's helping you or not until the very last moment.

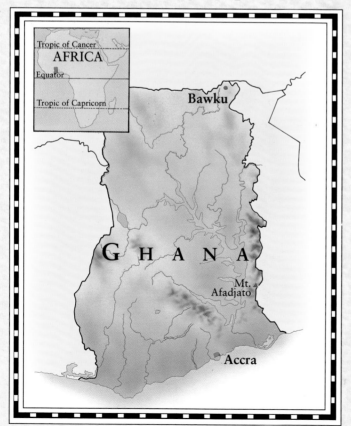

*The ancient kingdom of Ghana, where the story of Anansi was first told, didn't occupy the same area as the Ghana we see on a map today. Many modern African borders have only been decided very recently.*

# Anansi and Hate-to-be-Contradicted

**T**here was a man called Hate-to-be-Contradicted. People gave him that name because he was very bad-tempered and always disagreed with people.

One morning a friend called on Hate-to-be-Contradicted, and they sat in the shade of his palm tree. As they were talking, some palm nuts pattered to the ground.

"Hate-to-be-Contradicted, your palm nuts are ripe," the friend said.

"They are not ripe yet."

"Yes, some have fallen. Look how ready for picking they are."

"They are not ripe."

The friend was puzzled. Some more palm nuts fell.

"See, more ripe palm nuts!"

Hate-to-be-Contradicted was being contradicted. He grew red. He shouted.

"They are not ready. They will be ready when I am ready to say they are. They will be ready long before you know anything about palm nuts. When palm nuts are really ripe, all the bunches on a branch open at the same time with a sudden loud noise like a charging rhino. Then they tumble down on the head of anyone who disagrees with me. What do you think of that?"

"I think you are making too much fun of your friend."

"And I sell them all and buy a house for my old grandmother, and in that she gives birth to my mother, who gives birth to me, and I say hello to myself as soon as I'm born. What do you think of that?"

"I think you are a stupid liar who tells ridiculous stories and is very rude indeed to your friend," the friend said.

Hate-to-be-Contradicted went mad. "You disagreeing person! People who contradict me deserve a beating! How dare you!" he screamed, flying at his friend with a stick, driving him out of his courtyard.

Hate-to-be-Contradicted also hit his neighbor with a broom when he disagreed about whose dog had the fewest fleas. Then he tipped a brother-in-law into a well for not agreeing that the moon was made of curdled cows' milk. And he threw his cooking pot at a visitor for saying that the sun rose over his village before it rose over Hate-to-be-Contradicted's village.

The head man of the village decided to consult the clever Anansi. Perhaps he could stop the fights and beatings.

Anansi said he would go to see Hate-to-be-Contradicted.

It was the time of year again when the palm nuts were ripe. "Good morning, Hate-to-be-Contradicted, how are you this fine day?" Anansi asked.

Anansi and Hate-to-be-Contradicted sat under the palm tree talking, and again some ripe palm nuts fell. And again Hate-to-be-Contradicted told his story about how to tell when palm nuts were really ripe.

"What do you think of that?" asked Hate-to-be-Contradicted.

"I know what you say is true," Ananasi said. "I myself have often heard the sound of palm nut bunches opening. But you must come to my farm and see my sweet potato trees. They are so tall I have to tie ten sticks together end-to-end to reach them. Even then they are too far away, so I take my bow and arrows and shoot them down one by one. What do you think of that?"

Hate-to-be-Contradicted started to say, "Sweet potatoes do not. . ." when he stopped and gritted his teeth and said, "How interesting! I will come and see."

Anansi went home. On the path outside his house he sprinkled red palm juice. It looked like blood. Then he said to his children, "Hate-to-be-Contradicted is coming here. Tell him I broke my arm, and I'm at the blacksmith's having it hammered back on."

Hate-to-be-Contradicted arrived. The children said Anansi was at the blacksmith's having his arm mended and took him outside to see the splashes of blood where it broke.

"That's ridic. . ." Hate-to-be-Contradicted started to say —and stopped. He was furious that Anansi was not there, but had to control his temper. "Isn't your mother at home either?" he asked.

The children of Anansi could weave wonderful stories of their own.

"When our mother was on her way to the stream today," the youngest said, "she dropped her water pot. While it was falling she remembered she'd left something cooking and came home to take the pan off the fire. Now she's gone back to the stream to finish catching the water pot."

Hate-to-be-Contradicted was beside himself with fury, but held it in. Then Anansi came back and invited Hate-to-be-Contradicted to share their meal. The children served a tiny fish on a pile of furiously hot peppers. Hate-to-be-Contradicted took one mouthful. He felt as if his mouth had burst into flames.

"Water!" he gasped. "Please, Anansi, water!"

Anansi said calmly to his oldest child, "Bring some water for our guest's furiously burning hot mouth."

A minute later the child came back, without water.

"I am very sorry," Anansi's oldest child said. "There is no water. The three layers of water in the pot belong to others. The water at the top is father's, the middle layer of water is for our mother, and grandmother drinks the lowest layer. So there is none left."

Hate-to-be-Contradicted exploded. "You lying
offspring of a crocodile's stinking breath and. . ."

"Now, Mr. Hate-to-be-Contradicted," Anansi said
calmly, "you are contradicting us. We shall beat you for
contradicting us. You have given other people a pile of
beatings for disagreeing with you. Now you get a heap of
beating yourself."

So Anansi and his family beat this flinty man Hate-to-
be-Contradicted so hard he broke into pieces, and the
pieces broke into smaller pieces and scattered and were
worn down to fine grains of Hate-to-be-Contradicted that
blew into everything and found their way everywhere.
And that is why there is a little bit of Hate-to-be-
Contradicted in everybody.

# ASHANTI

When an Ashanti storyteller performs a tale, he often starts by saying: "Now this story—I didn't make it up!" The audience says: "Who did then?" And at the end, the storyteller says: "Now that is my story—and whether it is sweet or not sweet, take a bit of it and keep the rest under your pillow."

Ashanti people, who live in a region of Ghana, tell many stories about the hairy monster Sasabonsam. He has long thin legs—so thin they can be mistaken for creepers or twigs, so thin that other creatures might swing on them or try to pick them up . . . sometimes with unfortunate results.

Sasabonsam breathes fire and smoke, exactly like a dragon, and his feet face backward. So it's easy to spot him. . .

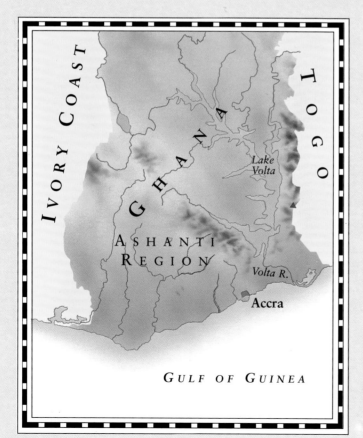

*The territory of the ancient Ashanti Empire in the eighteenth and nineteenth centuries stretched across what is now southern Ghana, from the Kanoé River in the west to the Togo Mountains in the east.*

# The Monster Sasabonsam versus the Wonder Child

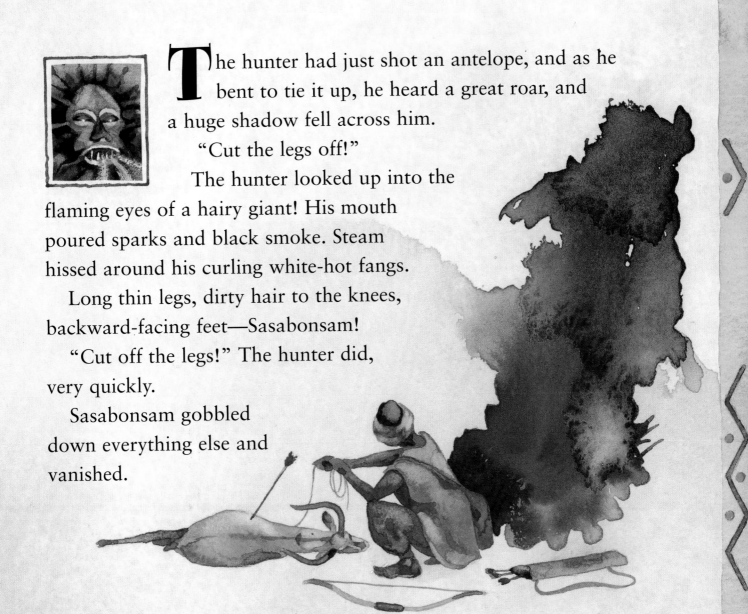

**T**he hunter had just shot an antelope, and as he bent to tie it up, he heard a great roar, and a huge shadow fell across him.

"Cut the legs off!"

The hunter looked up into the flaming eyes of a hairy giant! His mouth poured sparks and black smoke. Steam hissed around his curling white-hot fangs.

Long thin legs, dirty hair to the knees, backward-facing feet—Sasabonsam!

"Cut off the legs!" The hunter did, very quickly.

Sasabonsam gobbled down everything else and vanished.

The next day, and every day after, the same thing happened. The hunter's wife decided to find out why he brought home so little meat. She drilled a hole in his powder box and followed its leaking trail. It was hard work for her because she was pregnant. But she found him—and waited.

A black duiker came along. Bang! Then a thundering voice—"Cut off its legs!" The wife looked up into a huge mouth spitting red-hot cinders—and fainted.

"The legs!" This time Sasabonsam was pointing at the hunter's wife, lying behind the tree. The hunter was paralyzed with fear. "The legs!" The hunter couldn't move. Sasabonsam reached to grab the hunter's wife.

As soon as he touched her, the baby inside her leaped out, dribbling fire and purple smoke. He grew six feet a second and in next to no time he was Sasabonsam's size. He grabbed a tree. Boing! on Sasabonsam's ear. Sasabonsam hurled a rock. Boing! The forest shook. Snakes hissed away at top speed.

The fight went back and forth, one on top, then the other.

Sprawling on the floor, the Child Wonder saw a little metal hammer on Sasabonsam's belt. He clutched at it and hit Sasabonsam on the nose. The monster reeled. He stretched upward screeching: "Sky-god Nana Nyamee Kwame, one of your children has attacked me!"

But Sasabonsam couldn't reach Sky-god. He tottered and fell, and spilled hissing everywhere, and became a huge river.

The "baby"—his name was Akokoaa Kwasi Gyinamoa —shrank back into his mother and patiently waited to be born.

# YORUBA

In southwest Nigeria, towns are full of the flowing robes of Yoruba men and the brilliant dresses of Yoruba women. The Yoruba are an imaginative people, in their "talking drum" music, their poems about animals, their beautiful sculptures, and their legends and stories.

Yoruba stories are full of demons and spirits. In the forest, especially, skeletons dance, skulls talk, ogres eat people—for the forest is where the human soul lives after death. Some people still lock their doors at night and don't go out in case they meet a ghost. Ghosts can cause madness; people who meet them talk to themselves forever, without making sense. The most frightening thing about ghosts, though, is their taste for human flesh. . .

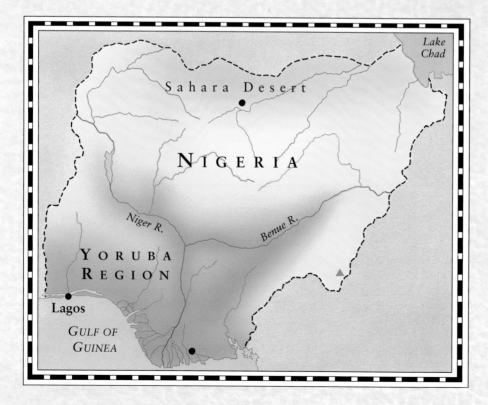

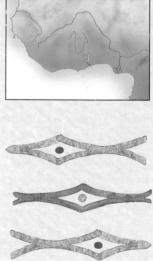

*The Yoruba people live mainly in the southwestern part of Nigeria.*

# Down to Deadtown

**T**he young couple had been married for a year, and the wife had not seen her parents in all that time.

"I miss my mother and father," she said to her husband. "Now that you have finished harvesting the corn, can we go to see them?"

"I want to see them too," her young husband said. "I will come with you."

They set off. To get to the home of her parents, which was in another part of the country, they had to cross a shallow river. At the riverbank, they heard a voice.

"Please, carry me over the river." They saw what spoke: a skull on a rock.

The young man and his wife held each other's hands tightly.

"Take me across the river."

"If we don't carry it across it might harm us," the wife said. "We can leave it at the other side."

The husband picked up the skull by the gaping mouth and waded into the river. He felt a pain in his hand. The skull was gripping hard! He tried to shake it off into the water. The skull bit deeper and clung harder.

"Put me on your shoulder. I'm getting wet."

The man lifted the skull to his shoulder like a pot. The skull gripped hard on his fingers. They reached the other side.

"Turn into the forest. Do as I tell you. Or I will bite your neck."

The man shuddered.

"Turn in along this path."

"But we are going to my wife's parents and the sun is already setting. . ." There was a searing hot pain in his neck. The young husband turned into the darkening forest.

The skull led them, adjusting its grip on the man's neck to make him turn. They walked till the light suddenly faded as the sun went down.

They were deep in the forest.

"Turn down here!" A steep rocky path spiraled downward alongside a river. The air turned cold. Bats came swirling up out of the dark, squeaking faintly for blood to drink. As the pair trudged on down through a stinking mist drifting off the stream, pale white flowers with dogs' faces reached toward them. Toadstools and huge funguses on clammy rocks by the path gazed up at them.

Finally, at the bottom, they came to a ruined village.

In a moment, there was a rustling noise, and ghostly shapes through which they could see the broken-down buildings came fluttering forward, shivering and reaching out to touch them, gibbering in scratchy whispers like dry leaves on a stone floor.

Deadtown! The skull had brought the young man and his wife to the Land of the Dead, where the ghosts ate human flesh!

"Go and collect wood for the fire," the skull said. "Don't try to run away. The dead are everywhere. And your blood scent is strong."

The terrified couple went back into the forest and started to collect wood. They were thinking hard how to escape, but what could they do? There was no way out.

They had nearly picked as much as they could carry. The woman bent to pick up her last piece of wood, which was covered in cobwebs. As she stooped, she saw dark eyes glittering up at her, the eyes of a handsome black spider.

"Please don't destroy my house!"

"We have to find wood for a fire," the young man said, keeping his voice down. "The dead are going to eat us.

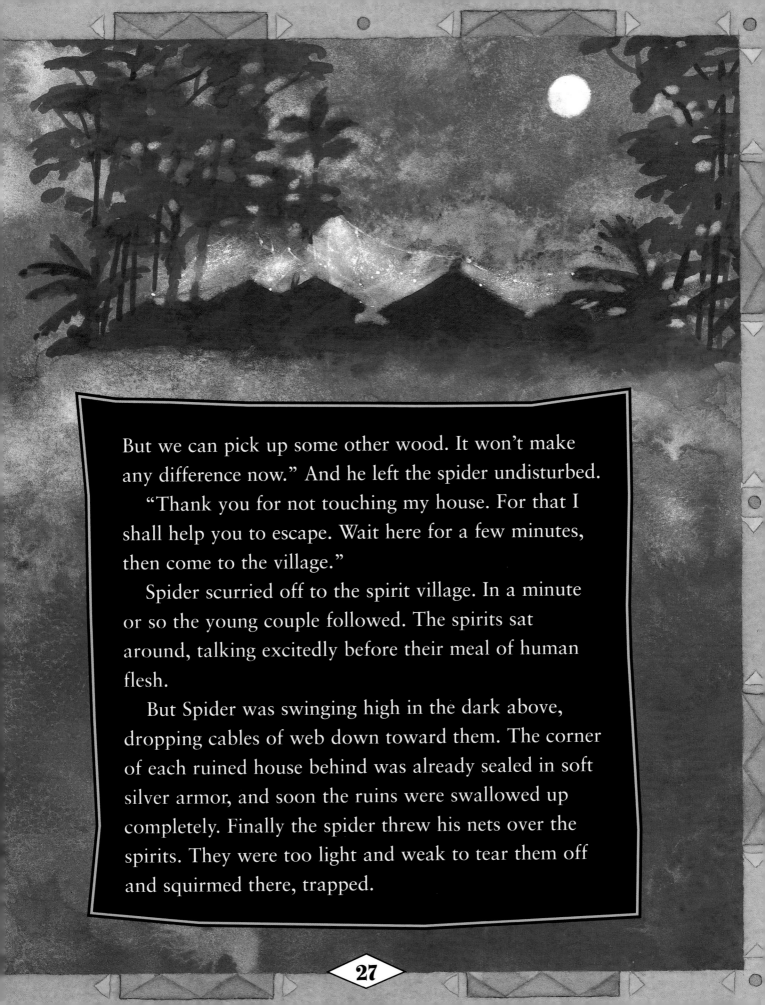

But we can pick up some other wood. It won't make any difference now." And he left the spider undisturbed.

"Thank you for not touching my house. For that I shall help you to escape. Wait here for a few minutes, then come to the village."

Spider scurried off to the spirit village. In a minute or so the young couple followed. The spirits sat around, talking excitedly before their meal of human flesh.

But Spider was swinging high in the dark above, dropping cables of web down toward them. The corner of each ruined house behind was already sealed in soft silver armor, and soon the ruins were swallowed up completely. Finally the spider threw his nets over the spirits. They were too light and weak to tear them off and squirmed there, trapped.

"You are safe. You can go now," Spider said.

"But which way?" the man asked. "We are lost." They had no idea how to escape from the forest. "Very well, I'll show you the way. Wait," Spider said, and swung up into the trees. They watched him climb swiftly up through the dark trees and out of sight. In a few minutes Spider's woven rope was swinging beside them. They took hold and began to climb, up and up. It was exhausting and terrifying; every creeper dangling against their faces might be the hairy Sasabonsam monster's legs. Monkeys shrieked at them and cinder-eyed thick black snakes watched them go past. But they climbed right to the top, where Spider was waiting.

"We're at the top. Follow me
along the path out of the forest," he
said. "Keep hold of this rope so that we
don't get separated in the dark and take a
wrong turn." Through the thick darkness they
held the spider's rope till they came to the
light again, to fields with animals and crops,
the land of the living.

"Will you come with us to our home, so that
we can reward you for helping us?" the young
woman asked.

Spider went with them. When they got back
home the young man said, "You gave us our
home back, so you can treat it as your own if
you want to stay."

Spider found a nice
dark corner of their
house, and that's where
he is to this day.

# ANCIENT WEST AFRICA

Long before their history could ever be recorded, there were great cities in West Africa. Word of them only reaches us through rumor, whispering through time of the kingdoms of Kanem-Bornu, ancient Ghana, and Timbuktu. These cities have long since been overrun by the desert or the jungle, but legends about them still survive. Once in a while, new facts come to light that suggest the old legends are true: in Mali in 1914 archaeologists found ruins of an ancient city—perhaps ancient Ghana.

Gassire was the son of a legendary king who came from the north and settled with his people along the Niger River. Legend says, over the centuries, his people built four cities, all of which disappeared. Perhaps the story of the four cities that disappeared came from the migration of Gassire's people south to the Niger, building and living in different cities.

Or maybe, as the legend says, four cities rose and fell in the same place.

REGION OF THE
WEST AFRICAN KINGDOMS

*The ancient West African kingdoms have given their names to today's rivers, cities, and even countries.*

# The First City of Wagudu

**I**n the ancient city of Wagudu was a prince named Gassire, who was a great warrior. The armies of a hostile tribe, the Burdama, had been attacking the city. Gassire had killed many of their princes single-handedly.

Gassire's father, the king, was old and frail. Gassire wanted to be king instead. But when the wise man of the court was asked if Gassire would be king, he made a strange prophecy.

"Gassire will never be king. The city will fall, and you will wander in the fields. You will no longer fight and kill. You will only sing about fighting and killing."

Sick at heart, Gassire went into the fields. He heard a woodcock singing. It sang a few terrible words, about the fall of a city. *"The city will fall, men will die, but my song will live forever."* As he rode home, the song haunted him: *"The city will fall, men will die, but my song will live forever."*

Gassire asked for a lute to be made for him. When the instrument-maker brought it, Gassire touched the strings. They were silent.

"The lute will not speak for me."

"It cannot speak," the instrument-maker said. "It is only wood and strings. It has no heart, no experience. Take it into battle. There it will hear the cries of the dying and the clash of swords. Then it will speak."

Next day, his lute hanging from his shoulder, Gassire rode out to fight the Burdama. With him went his eight sons and hundreds of young men of Wagudu. There was a terrible battle. Gassire killed many Burdama, but his own eldest son was killed, and many other young Wagudu men. As Gassire carried his eldest son home on his horse, his blood dripped down onto the lute.

The following day was the same. Gassire killed more of the Burdama, but another son died, and more young men. The battling went on for five days, until in the evening Gassire came home with only one son, his youngest, and a handful of young Wagudu men still ready to fight along with him the next day.

On that same evening people came to Gassire.

"We beg you to end this terrible fighting. Take your horses and men, your swords and spears, and leave us. Leave the city in peace."

Gassire and his son, and his few followers and their wives and children, rode far out into the emptiness beyond the city. They camped and lit their fires in the fields where Gassire had heard the woodcock sing.

The flames dwindled down. The big stars came out. Gassire was awake. He heard a fingering of strings, played without a hand.

The lute itself sang the story of Wagudu. It remembered the din of battle and the terrible cries of the dying. The blood of Gassire's seven sons had flowed into it. It sang from the heart. In the music was the fall of Wagudu, the stench of decay, but also the peace of the fields and the birds singing:

"They let the Burdama come. They would not defend their city.

"The Burdama broke into the city, the lost city of Wagudu, where sand blows among the fallen stones.

"They plundered and killed. There was no one left alive. Not a wall was left standing."

The lute sang the tale of a terrible future too.

"This was the end of the first city. There are still three cities of Wagudu, with gates facing the four winds, yet to rise and be destroyed. Not a wall of any will be left standing. Owls will call from their ruins. Sand will blow over their fallen stones."

# A MANY-TONGUED LAND

Perhaps it isn't surprising to find a story about language in a land of many languages. This next story was (and is) told in the Akan language, one of the many spoken in Ghana. Ghana is a land of different peoples and places too, with hot, wet forests in the south, and in the north hot, dry grassland—"savanna."

Some things are the same all over Ghana. Marvelous stories are told everywhere. Animals and magic nearly always appear in them. Spiders climb to heaven and pythons stretch from horizon to horizon. Leopards and monkeys marry human beings. And they all talk. When mice talk, they are very interesting, because they know everything about human beings.

But animals and people should really keep their distance. . .

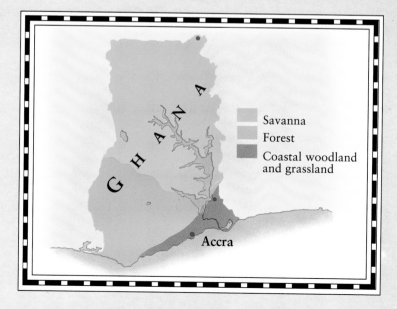

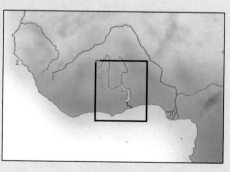

*Ghana's range of habitats means that it is home to many different kinds of animals.*

# The Man who Learned the Language of Animals

**O**hia was unlucky with his farming. Birds ate his corn, monkeys dug up his cassava, and his hens laid their eggs where he couldn't find them. Everything Ohia tried went wrong.

With nothing to sell, and hardly anything to eat, he and his wife Ariwehu became poor and hungry. Ariwehu complained that her clothes were worn out.

Ohia decided he would ask his rich neighbor if there was any work he could do.

"You can cut down those coconut palm trees for me," the neighbor said.

"Can I take the sap from the trees to make palm wine?"

"You can. I will lend you pots to collect the sap, but I would like a share of the wine you make."

So they agreed. In two days Ohia cut down his neighbor's trees, and when they were lying on the ground he cut the bark to make the sap flow. Then he positioned the pots to collect the sap.

37

Exhausted, Ohia went home for a good sleep, but instead of sleeping, he lay awake listening to the sap dribbling into his pots. He thought of all the palm wine that Ariwehu would sell at the market and of all the money she would bring home.

In the morning he took his biggest pot and went to collect the sap.

Every pot was broken, every drop of sap gone!

Ohia went home in despair, but Ariwehu said, "Some blundering creature has broken your pots accidentally. Borrow some more, and try again."

So Ohia borrowed more pots and put them in place. But he decided to watch the pots that night, just in case....

The dark came, and a moon rose. Ohia shivered. Every small sound was a ghost creeping up to touch him. Then he saw a shape glide along the path and stop by his trees. He listened hard. There was a lapping sound, then crack!—a pot broke. He ran forward. A deer! The thief was a deer, carrying her own large collecting pot. The deer saw him and shied off. Ohia ran after her. He ran and ran, the deer with the pot on her back leaping ahead on a twisting path uphill through the moonlit forest.

Eventually the deer, exhausted, ran out into a large clearing where there were many animals lying sleepily around a kingly leopard. Ohia stopped. If all these creatures were the deer's friends . . . perhaps the deer was thieving for them.

The deer gasped out a story to the leopard, about being hunted and chased. But the kingly leopard courteously asked Ohia for his version of the story. Ohia apologized for chasing the deer and trespassing in the land of animals. Then he told his story from the beginning, about how unlucky he had been as a farmer, and how poor he and Ariwehu were, then about his pots being broken and the sap taken.

"The deer is a thief. We creatures apologize for her. To make amends we shall replace the pots and also offer you a gift that will make you rich. When you return home you will be able to understand the language of animals. But you must never reveal your gift. If you do, you will die. Go now."

Ohia went home. The next day his pots were full to overflowing. He made palm wine, and Ariwehu sold it. They started to make a little money. Ariwehu wore nice dresses. Their hard work was being rewarded, but they were not rich. But then they had a son, which made them feel rich.

Ohia got used to hearing creatures talk. Often it was no more interesting than "What shall we eat today?" or "We shall have a storm this afternoon." But one morning Ohia was looking around for hen's eggs, when he heard one cluck with disapproval as he went past them scratching in the dirt.

"That halfwit, wandering around looking for eggs."

"Imagine working, ugh."

"With a pot of gold buried behind his house."

What the hen said was true. Ohia found the gold and became the richest man in the village. He decided to buy a second wife. Then he would be even more important and respected.

Ohia's new wife was beautiful
but very jealous of Ariwehu.
She didn't like Ariwehu and
Ohia being together and
tried to listen to everything
they said. She hated it when
they laughed together, and
thought they were making fun
of her.

One evening Ohia and Ariwehu were
sitting quietly, not saying anything because the new wife
was near, when Ohia heard two mice talking.

"They'll be going to bed soon. We can wait a few
minutes."

"Those bean cakes. Mouth-watering. They'll last the
week if we're careful."

Ohia laughed out loud.

The second wife came storming up to Ohia. "What are
you laughing at? Why do you and Ariwehu make fun of
me all the time? I hate you!"

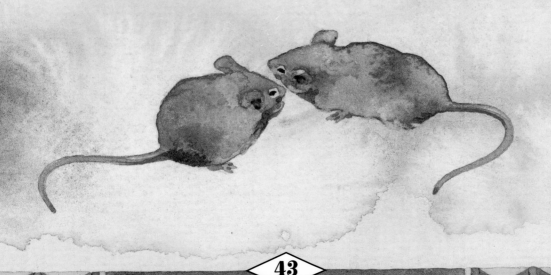

With all the jealousy and quarreling, Ohia's life became a misery. One day the second wife's fury became uncontrollable, and she attacked Ariwehu with a knife. Ohia had to ask the village head man what he should do.

"Tell me everything that has happened. Everything."

Ohia knew that his life was over. He would soon have to tell the whole story. He arranged a feast, with dancing and storytelling and music—and much palm wine. Ohia heard a hen cluck to a friend, "These are the most scraps we've ever had."

As the feast neared its end, Ohia announced he had a story to tell. He told about his bad luck, the stolen sap, and the chase, and at the moment when he told everyone about the gift of the language of animals, he fell to the earth, dead.

There was lamenting and wailing, as the feast became a funeral. The jealous second wife, who had driven Ohia from the world, was driven from the village. She died, and her jealous ashes were scattered to the four winds, which took them and scattered jealousy throughout the world.

# Glossary

**Anansi spiderman** A favorite trickster character in Ghanaian and West Indian stories, who is human and spider at the same time. He cheats and schemes. He is lazy. He has a lisp. Even when he dies in a story, he's there again in the next tale.

**Bats** Some Africans believe the souls of the dead flutter about as bats.

**Duiker** A kind of antelope.

**Gassire** The exploits of the hero Gassire are told in the first part of a great story called the Dausi. Gassire was supposed to have composed and performed the whole story, as well as his own part. The performer would have sung it from memory, accompanying himself on a stringed instrument.

**Ghosts** Ghosts in African stories eat people, carving them up with a huge thumbnail, so their nails smell. They can speak human language and cause madness.

**Lute** A musical instrument a bit like the guitar, but smaller, and with a more rounded sound box.

**Sasabonsam** A long-legged hairy giant monster from the jungle. He has feet that point backward. Cunning characters—like Anansi, Hare, or Tortoise—easily outwit monsters.

**Savanna** The hot, dry grassland that stretches across West Africa in the northern part of Nigeria and Ghana.

# Books to Read

Arnott, Kathleen. *African Myths and Legends*. New York: Oxford University Press, 1990.

Ardagh, Philip. *African Myths and Legends*. New York: Dillon Press, 1998.

Barnett, Jeannie. *Ghana* (Major World Nations). Broomall, PA: Chelsea House, 1998.

Bennett, Martin. *West African Trickster Tales* (Oxford Myths and Legends). New York: Oxford University Press Children's, 1994.

Courlander, Harold. *Treasury of African Folklore: The Oral Literature, Traditions, Myths, Legends, Epics, Tales, Recollections, Wisdom, Sayings, and Humor of Africa*. New York: Marlowe and Company, 1995.

Greene, Rebecca L. *The Empire of Ghana* (First Book). Danbury, CT: Franklin Watts, 1998.

McKissack, Patricia and McKissack, Frederick. *The Royal Kingdoms of Ghana, Mali, and Songhay: Life in Medieval Africa*. New York: Henry Holt, 1995.

# West Africa Activities

The character of Anansi is great fun to use as a character in your own stories. Once you have read a few Anansi tales, and know the kind of person he is, you can invent your own.

∞

You might enjoy turning "Anansi and Hate-to-be-Contradicted" into a play, and video recording it. It would also sound good on audiotape.

∞

It might be nice and creepy to tell the Deadtown story from the skull's point of view. "I was waiting on a rock by a river. . ." Maybe you could write about Spider's new life. Spider would be the "I" of the story.

∞

Gassire becomes a poet, who sings songs on his lute. Could you write some of his songs? And perhaps perform them on the guitar—similar to a lute. They would probably be very sad at times, but not always.

∞

Finally, you could write a story of your own about a human being who is given the power to understand the language of animals. Stories using this idea occur all over the world.